This book given in love to

_____

By _____

On _____

Dearest Reader,

Psalm 119:28 says:
My soul is weary with Sorrow; strengthen
me according to your word.
Put your hope and trust in Christ
And in His word. He loves you,
oh how He loves you !!
You are His most precious and
beloved child. He will Always
Love you - FOREVER.

Jen Campbell

Hosea 10:12

# The Story of Gomer

## From the Book of Hosea

# Geri Campbell

We want to hear from you. Has this book touched your life? Send your comments to instepministries@yahoo.com.

For information regarding Geri Campbell and her ministry, including requests for a live presentation of the play *The Story of Gomer* and speaking events, as well as available scripts, performance rights, and DVDs, please visit

www.in-stepministries.com

To my heavenly Bridegroom

I'm watching for You

# Contents

## Part 2, Geri's Story

## Part 3, Your Story

## Part 4, The End of the Story

# Acknowledgments

First, let me say there is truly no way to properly thank or acknowledge the countless people who have helped and encouraged me in this project, and throughout my ministry. Getting the play *The Story of Gomer* off the ground was a tremendous challenge in and of itself, and a huge amount of gratitude goes out to Richard Kearny, Stephen Tedeschi, my mom-time group, Sue Ann Cordell, Lakeshore Christian Church, and many others who gave so much to us in the early years.

Speaking of early years, very special thanks go to you, Mrs. Jane Sherman. You cast me as Heidi in our third grade classroom play, and the rest is history. I'll never forget the day, 30 years later, when you came to see *The Story of Gomer,* and the joy that we shared in finding out we were both believers in Christ.

Thank you, Michael Culhane, my high school drama and English teacher, for always believing in me and calling me your "shining star".

Sharee Lemos, my director in Syracuse for so many years, I learned so much from you. You gave me a shot at a really big role when I was 17, and I'm not sure I'd be where I am today if you hadn't taken a chance on me. Thank you for shaping me as an actress and as a person. I hope you know how much you mean to me.

To Dell Hubbard, if it were not for you, I probably would not have written this book. Thank you for your obedience to God and your generosity when you blessed me with a laptop computer. I knew I could not look at that brand new laptop and NOT write this book!

Thank you to my dear editor Ellen Horton, who spent countless hours reading and editing my manuscript. Thank you for giving this project your time and devotion and asking nothing in return. You are my sweet sister in Christ.

Thank you to Doug Henderson and Deb Minnard for your amazing creative talents for the cover art and photos. Both of you are true servants of Christ. God has greatly used you, and I am blessed to be your friend.

Thank you to many of our family and friends who have given so much to us over the years. Every time I wanted to quit, God sent someone to take my hand to help me in the next step of the journey. Thanks to Christine, Maria, Connie, Ronda, Cheryl, Pat, and others who have blessed us in countless ways.

Thank you to Dr. Meyer and the staff at Valley Forge Christian College for being the real life inspiration for Chapter Eleven. I'll never forget what you did that day!

To Rich's parents, Marvin and Judy Campbell, thank you for opening your home to our family when God led us to leave Nashville; and thanks for watching the kids countless times and allowing us to travel with our ministry. We would never be able to do what we do without you.

To my father, Robert J Stepien, thank you for allowing me to tell your story. I remember that, after your aneurism, you wished you could make an impact on people for Christ but it was "too late". Well, it's never too late, and now your life and your story will touch more lives than you could ever have imagined. I love you, Dad.

To my wonderful, extraordinarily beautiful and talented mother Christine Gancarz, what words can possibly express gratitude for all you have done for me? You have told me every day of my life that I am strong, that I am beautiful, and that I can do anything I put my mind to. You instilled a confidence in me that is invaluable. Mommy, you are the wind beneath my wings.

To my kids, thank you for putting up with me. It's not always easy to live with me when I'm writing, so thank you for loving me and understanding when Mom has the door closed. Mercy, my dear daughter, thanks for helping me develop my characters and for editing my work. Your insights are way beyond your years.

Thank you to my amazing husband Rich Campbell, you are my true Hosea. Thank you for teaching me what it means to be a servant. Thank you for all you do for our ministry and our family. God was right; I can never be all that I am meant to be without you. I love you, Sir Richard.

Mostly, thanks to my Lord and Savior Jesus Christ. Thanks for never giving up on me. Thank You for revealing Your heart to me. I am, and always will be, Yours.

Have you ever wondered
what God would say to you,
if He could?
What if,
for some reason,
God could only say
one sentence
that you could hear,
what do you think He would say?

# Part 1

# Gomer's Story

1

# Present Day Life

Israel 785 BC

*"For I know the plans I have for you," declares the Lord, "plans to prosper you and not to harm you, plans to give you hope and a future."* Jeremiah 29:11

My name is Gomer. I know what you are thinking, strange name for a woman. My name means *complete*. I have to tell you, though, only in recent years have I come to understand and own my name. Perhaps a better description would be incomplete, for I have spent most of my life searching for something or someone to fill an empty void in my life.

What? Yes, I am talking to you. And yes, I know that a writer is not supposed to address her audience in a book. The lady who is writing my story down for me has read all kinds of books on how to write books. See, I just used the same word twice in a sentence, and now she is mad at me. But this is my story, and I am going to tell it the way I want to tell it, and if you don't like it you can just put the book down.

Sorry, the old me still comes out sometimes. I've never been known for my meekness or gentleness. But this is serious business. And you might think I don't know you, but I do. Of

3

course, it is presumptuous to say, but I do not think we are so different from one another. You want to be loved, and you want to give love, but your heart is just a little bit broken. Maybe it is a lot broken...

I have to stop right here and be honest.

I don't want to do this. I want to walk away right now and let you remember me as a dedicated wife and loving mother.

People who meet me for the first time think I have it all together. When they tell me of their struggles and trials, and I say that I understand, they laugh at me. They say, "Ha! What do you know of heartache and pain? Look at your life; it's perfect!" They think I am someone who has it all together.

If you look at me right now, you'll see I am surrounded by love. I have a comfortable home, beautiful children and grandchildren, and a wonderful husband. It would be so much easier to just let you think that I have, and have always had, a perfect life.

Some may think, what's the point? Why bother bringing up the past? All that matters is where you are today. And yes, in a way, that is true. I do not bring up the past to condemn myself—God knows I have spent way too much time doing that. But, rather, I remember with a grateful heart all God has brought me through. I find that keeps me from taking my present life for granted.

But oh, yes, there is a much bigger reason I feel the need to tell my story.

I cannot ignore this burning in my heart to tell you about my life. All I can think about is that perhaps there is someone out there, right now, just like me, who doesn't understand forgiveness. What if there is a broken heart, a shattered person who feels completely alone in what they are going through?

Well, you are not alone. I've been there, too. Once I had strayed so far away from my home, from all that I loved, that I thought there was no way I could ever return. So, it is for you that I tell my story, because God has put an ache in my heart for you.

What's more, God Himself loves you more than you will ever, ever know, and He has sent me here to tell you...

There is always a way back home.

## Chapter Two

# Childhood Dreams

*"Before I formed you in the womb I knew you..."*
Jeremiah 1:5a

"Hannah, Hannah, wait for me!" Breathless, we duck around the corner of an old stone house, safe from the boys who are hurling stones at us. Bent over from exhaustion, Hannah and I try to catch our breath, but start laughing before we can get air into our lungs.

"Those dumb boys, they better stop throwing rocks at us or I'll tell!" I barely get the words out when Hannah picks up a small stone and steps out from behind our protective wall. Giggling, she throws the rock.

"What are you doing, Hannah? Don't throw the rock back!"

"Why?" Hannah quickly leaps sideways to safety.

"Because they'll think we like them." Didn't Hannah know anything?

"Why would they think that?" Hannah now gave me her full attention.

"Because my mother told me boys are only mean to the girls they like." My mother didn't really have to tell me that because I already knew. The man who is with my mom all the time is mean to her, and he says he loves her. My father was never mean to my mother, and now he is gone, but I didn't feel like telling Hannah all that so I just said, "I know! You like Abner! You threw the rock because you like Abner!"

"Well..." Hannah tries to think of something smart to say. "Well, you like Hosea!"

"I do not like Hosea," I mutter, turning my back to her. "I don't like any boys, especially not Hosea. I wouldn't marry Hosea if he were the last boy in the whole wide world!"

Hannah lets out a laugh. I love that I can always make her laugh.

"And anyway, if I do ever get married," I continue, "I'm going to marry a handsome king, and he'll take me away to live with him in a big, beautiful palace. And he'll have a really pretty horse."

"I love horses," Hannah sighs. She loves this story, and although I have told it many times before, she still acts as though it is the first time she's heard it.

"And he is going to love me forever and ever, and buy me lots of stuff," I say, reaching for Hannah's hand. I love this story as much as I love Hannah.

"I can come too, 'cause I'm your..."

"Very best friend!" we say together.

Taking both of Hannah's hands, I assure her, "Yes, you are my very best friend, and we'll marry good men who will never hurt us, and we'll live in palaces right next to each other."

"We'll always be best friends and…" Hannah's words are cut short as her mother calls for her.

"I have to go, Gomer." Away she runs, leaving me hiding behind the wall all by myself.

I was all of seven years old, but I remember my dream of marrying a good man, and I remember hiding. Hiding. I am getting good at that. Rather, I should say, I am getting good at pretending. When I can't physically hide, I pretend inside my mind and go hide somewhere else.

It is what I do when I perform at the temple. At first it was fun. It feels good when the people clap. I like all the attention, and I sure get a lot of attention, especially from the men. It is creepy because they are old, but they tell me I am pretty like my mother, and I like that.

Dancing is fun, but lately it feels weird, as though something inside my heart says, "Don't do it." The older girls don't seem to mind, and I want to be just like the older girls. My mom is proud of me. She shows me off, but I don't care.

I have a show tonight. Lately, I have been performing every night. Less time to play, more time to learn new steps and stage directions. If I make a mistake, I get in trouble, and the man that is always with my mother yells at her. I will make sure I do everything perfectly tonight so she doesn't get yelled at.

I hope that I do not have to keep this up. I hope that sometime I can just play with Hannah and not worry about all this.

And I hope I marry a king.

## Chapter Three

# Teen Rebellion

*"The Lord is slow to anger, abounding in love and forgiving sin and rebellion."* Numbers 14:18a

"Okay, Okay, Hannah, they are right over there. How do I look? Is there anything in my teeth?"

Hannah just smiles at me. I know I look like a horse with huge flapping lips, baring its teeth.

"How do I look?" Hannah coos the question in her sweet, quiet voice.

"You look beautiful. You always do. I have to admit, I think it funny that we are chasing the very boys who used to chase us and throw rocks," I say as I ponder how to get their attention.

Hannah waits for my instructions.

"I know!" I suddenly hit upon a brilliant idea. "Let's walk a little farther down the hill, and we can get a better view, and they can get a better view, and we will pretend we are totally not interested. Then when I give you the signal, you turn around and tell me if Abner is looking at me, okay?"

"Okay." Hannah never hesitates to go with my plans.

We walk arm in arm down the hill, closer to the boys, and I see that Abner is indeed there. I can hardly breathe; he is so gorgeous.

"Now, when I give you the signal, you turn around...No, Hannah, not yet! Why did you look? You looked too soon, and now he totally knows I like him."

Hannah stands there, perplexed. "He wasn't looking, anyway."

"What do you mean he wasn't looking anyway?" I stomp around, trying to understand why the love of my life isn't looking at me. "I can't believe he wasn't looking. He doesn't even notice me. Was Joseph looking?"

Hannah shakes her head.

"Was Eli looking?"

She shakes her head again.

"Was, like, anyone looking?"

This time I get a nod yes. "Hosea. Hosea was looking." Hannah seems amused.

"Ugh, it figures, the only one I *don't* want to notice me."

"Why do you not want Hosea to notice you? Gomer, he is a nice boy, a good boy."

"Because Hosea is *always* looking at me! It is so totally creepy, and he is not exactly much to look at. He always has his nose stuck in a scroll, and he probably thinks he is smarter than everyone else. Everywhere I go, when I see him, he seems to stare right through me. I can't stand it!"

Hannah, ever so sweet says, "I feel sorry for him. You are right, he is not much to look at, but…"

We notice that Hosea is on his way up the hill.

"Gomer, be nice to him." Hannah moves away and sits on a large rock, still within ear shot of us.

When Hosea approaches, I just can't look at him.

"Hi." Hosea kicks the small stones at his feet.

"Hi," I mumble, wishing Hannah would come over and take me away.

"How are you?" Apparently Hosea can't think of anything else to say.

"I'm fine," I respond. "At least, I *was* fine!"

"Um, I…I was wondering if you might allow me to court you. I was hoping you would…"

"No!" I shout louder than I intend to. "I mean, no thank you. I just don't feel that way about you, Hosea."

"Perhaps in time, you will come to love me." Hosea's voice cracks.

"Oh, please, trust me, it will not matter how much times passes, Hosea, I will never come to love you. I don't even like you. Now will you just, please, go away? You are blocking my view."

I can't help but notice the hurt look on his face or the way he seems to deflate right before my eyes, but I honestly don't care and I'm relieved to see him turn and slowly walk away.

Before I can say anything, Hannah takes my arm. "Why were you so rude to him? What did he do to deserve that?"

"I wasn't rude, I was honest." I am not used to Hannah standing up to me.

"Gomer, he is right, perhaps you can grow to love him." Hannah lets go of my arm, and takes my hand.

For some reason, I pull away in anger. "What? Love doesn't grow on you! What is it, like some kind of fungus or something? No, love is either there, or it's not. Love is that little feeling in your stomach, as though you're falling off a cliff; and you melt at the sound of his voice. Love is dreaming of the day he kisses you. Love makes you crazy, but it makes you feel alive, and I can't live without that kind of fun and excitement in my life. That is why I cannot marry Hosea."

Hannah falls silent.

"Oh Hannah, remember when we were little girls, and we used to dream we would marry handsome kings who would love us forever, and we would live in palaces right next to one another?" Even after all these years, Hannah still loves this story, except she doesn't seem to love it at the moment, for she walks away from me and heads for home.

"Hannah?" I run and stand in front of her.

"Gomer, I have something to tell you, but I just don't want to get into it right now."

"No, tell me now, Hannah. Please don't hide anything from me."

"I can't." She shifts her step to go around me.

"You're my best friend. You can tell me anything." I try not to

14

sound too upset, although I find my anger mounting. I am not used to this. People don't just walk away from me.

"Well, you know it is time for my father to choose my husband. He has chosen."

My mouth is open. "Who? Who has he chosen?"

Hannah almost whispers, "Amos."

"That guy who stands by the temple and shouts at everyone? 'Repent from your idols, one day God will punish Israel for her sins, God will destroy the altars of Bethel, blah blah blah.' That idiot Hosea is a friend of his, which is yet another reason I don't like Hosea."

"Gomer, my father has thrown all of our idols, including the goddess Astarte, out of our house. He has destroyed them all and repented in front of our whole family and to anyone who will listen. He talked to Amos and Hosea a couple weeks ago. When Amos said that our people Israel have forsaken the Lord our God by worshiping these false gods, my father just fell to his knees. It was really something."

"So, your father is just going to stop going to the temple of Astarte now? You know, I see him there a lot when I am performing. Well, now that you mention it, I have not seen him there recently, but I'm sure he will be back."

"No, no he won't, Gomer. The temple of Astarte is evil. Even our temple of the Lord at Bethel, where the people of Israel worship, is corrupt. At both places, the things that go on are an abomination to the Lord."

"Abomination? Listen to you, Hannah. These are Amos' words, not yours. And I suppose you are going to tell me my performing at the temple of Astarte is an abomination to God too, right?"

Hannah is trembling. "My father says we are moving closer to Bethel. He is going to speak against the temple there, and try to warn our people about the sin they are committing by their idol worship. And I will marry Amos. My father says that very few Godly men are available to marry. I'm sorry, Gomer."

I am stunned. "Fine! Marry whoever you want, but don't you condemn me! Your father has no right to judge me or what I do. He can sit there, performance after performance, and watch us with lustful eyes, and then all of a sudden he says it's wrong? All the Israelite men, they come and watch, and they pay their money. They are no different from the idol-worshiping men. You are right, Hannah, there are no more good men."

"Gomer, why don't you leave the temple of Astarte? Come with us." Hannah pleads with me.

Something wells up inside me. I can't even explain it. No one is going to tell me what to do. No one is going to tell me that the only thing I am good at is wrong.

"Then get out of here! Go marry that crazy man. And go ahead, condemn everyone in Israel. People are just going to laugh at you. That Amos is an embarrassment; so is Hosea. Have a nice life."

Then I run away. I just run. It is the last time I ever saw Hannah.

It is also the last time I cried.

After about an hour, I collect myself and wash my face. I redo my hair. I take a deep breath and never look back.

I have a show to do.

## Chapter Four

# Proposal to a Prostitute

*"... the old has gone, the new has come!"*
2 Corinthians 5:17b

I wait to go on. The drums beat a hypnotic rhythm, at first slow and steady, then increasing in tempo, whipping the crowd into a frenzy. The fires glow, and the people begin to cheer; they chant along with the lyrics. The women dancers file out and the crowd bursts forth with applause. The music is in full swing, and the altar is on fire.

Time to turn it on. I cannot do this on my own. I am no good on my own—it is not enough anymore. I raise my hands to the heavens, to the goddess Astarte, and ask her to fill me with her spirit. Come and bring me power. She enables me to do things I would never do on my own. I just let her take control, and when my time on stage is over, I don't even remember what I have done. As Yophe Raah says, it is just a character I play—just entertainment. More and more, Astarte, the goddess of promiscuity, has taken over. I pretend. I hide. Astarte is strong; she is vulgar, as she gives me power over men. My face contorts, and my body moves in ways I never thought possible. She thinks up seductive dance moves that can bring a man to his knees and make a good man forget about his God.

This is the life I have come to know, the life I have chosen. Anything I want is mine: fine wine, delicacies to eat, gold and pearls, beautiful clothing. However, with each year, I am pushed further to shock the crowd and keep them interested. Even Astarte struggles to inspire enough dark, disgusting moves to enable me to please them.

Yes, although I would never admit it to anyone, even I call it disgusting. A touch of the girl I used to be still lives inside the darkness of my heart; the real me has a conscience that causes me to realize the truth: I disgust myself.

Sometimes in the shadows of the night, after I have pleased some high ranking official or dignitary; or when Yophe Raah comes to me, I still dream that I marry a handsome man who will love me forever. He no longer has to be a king, for now I have known kings, and they do not love. I want a good man. A man that will not hurt me.

Once I thought I loved Yophe Raah. In fact, he told me that he would marry me one day.

"You are beautiful, Gomer." Yophe Raah caressed my face. "No one understands you like I do."

He is true to his name, *beautiful evil*, but I could not see it then.

"Let me take care of you. You have true talent. Let me make you into the woman we both know you can be. You'll have everything you could ever want. I love you, and I will never leave you."

I believed him. I thought he was the answer to everything. When my mother died, she was serving at the temple of the goddess Astarte. Since I had nowhere else to go, the temple was my only home. Everyone knew I danced there, and everyone knows that no good man will marry a girl who has served at that temple.

Yophe took me under his wing. At first, I didn't mind. I felt special. He was handsome and older than me, and all the ladies seemed to swoon over him. I told myself he really did love me, and I believed him when he said he would do what was best for me.

"Just try this costume, Gomer. I know you don't feel comfortable wearing it, but you look amazing. You'll have your outer cloak on to start with, and then, when you are comfortable, when you are ready, just take the cloak off." Yophe spoke in his pseudo-fatherly voice. "When the chanting grows louder, you will know that the crowd wants more." Yophe then turned away. "Of course, if you really don't want to, Diana is ready to take your place."

"No! No, I will do it. Don't give this role to Diana." I saw how Yophe looked at her. She had only been with us a short time, and he already had given her a leading role in another segment of the performance.

Yophe continued, "I also wanted to talk with you about something. I have a friend who is well connected politically. He is most lonely. I wonder if you would keep him company this evening. I'll be otherwise engaged and cannot entertain him. If you love me, you will do this."

I looked at him, fully understanding what he expected of me. The other women warned me that Yophe would start asking for favors, but I believed I was different. I believed Yophe would never want to share me.

"You know I love you." Yophe left my new costume with me and walked out. I heard him and Diana laughing outside my door, and a sinking feeling gripped my insides as I remembered my friend, the only friend I ever had say, "Leave the temple, Gomer, come with us…"

I made my choice at that time, entangling myself in the life that I now cannot escape.

My dreams are dead. I can only wish the same for myself. If only I could believe for one moment that there may be a way out of this misery...

Suddenly, I hear a commotion outside my window.

"'Their hearts are deceitful, and now they must bear their guilt. I am speaking to Israel. I will punish Israel for the days she worshiped false gods and burned incense to them. But me she forgot,' declares the Lord."

Someone is shouting in the street. Who would be bold enough to shout at the temple doorstep? The last man who did that was killed right on the temple stairs. This is either a man of courage or a man out of his mind. I run to the window to look. I catch my breath when I see him.

Hosea!

He's still not tall, dark, and handsome, but something undefined sets him apart. Something strong and confident, and so much like...home.

He doesn't back down from the people who mock him. He stands his ground and faces the angry mob dead on. Then he lowers his voice so much that I have to lean far out the window to hear him. Hosea's face softens, and in a gentle voice, rich with feeling, he says, "Therefore I am going to allure her; I will lead her into the desert and speak tenderly to her. There I will give her back her vineyards, and make the Valley of Distress a door of hope."

*A door of hope. Give her back her vineyards.* Sounds like a second chance!

20

Suddenly, Hosea turns and looks straight up at me. I catch myself, almost falling out of the window, lips frozen, eyes wide.

"I have come for you," is all he says.

I scurry down the stairs. He has come for me? What does he even mean by that? We have not seen each other in years. Why would he come for me? To chastise me, condemn me? Drag me out into the street and stone me? If this is the case, why am I running to meet him? My feet take me on their own; the rest of me is quite unwilling to travel down the stairs and out into the street. Before I know it, I stand, breathless, facing Hosea.

"What are you doing?" I try to ignore the numerous onlookers.

"I have come to ask you a question." Hosea has grown taller since I last saw him but still rather slight in build. Certainly, he wouldn't last long in a fight. However, something about the sound of his voice commands respect. At the same time, I find that voice to be soothing.

"A question?" Now he has me curious.

"Will you marry me?"

Speechless, I don't know what to do or how to respond. Surely he cannot be serious. No godly man would ever want me. Yes, once he wanted to marry me, once when I was a good girl, but not now. Not after all that I have done.

Then he does something remarkable. He touches me.

"No Hosea, you must not touch me. I am unclean. I am unclean!"

When I see his face and feel the gentleness of his touch, it hits me.

He still wants to marry me! *Me!*

Of all people, I am the most unworthy, unwanted…I am the most unlovable. Is it possible that there is a love so strong that it can overlook such a shameful past as mine? Oh, how I want to believe such a love exists!

"I'm waiting…" Hosea almost seems amused, as though he knows what I am going to say. That confidence annoys me.

Ha! Maybe he doesn't know what I am going to say. I could reject him—again. I don't need him. I am doing fine on my own, taking care of myself, thank you. I have a roof over my head, clothes on my back—quite nice ones, I might add. What need do I have of a…savior?

Oh, who am I kidding? Maybe what I truly fear is that I can never be what he wants me to be. Hosea deserves someone who is pure —pure in heart, pure in mind, and uh…pure in body. I can never give him that.

He knows this, and still he desires me? Does he think love can change me? Is that possible? Is there a love that beautiful, that… transforming? If a love like that exists, I want to find it. Oh, how I want to find it!

"I'm not leaving until you give me answer." Hosea still has my hand in his. I am lost in my thoughts for so long that even the most curious of onlookers has walked away.

"Um… YES! Yes, Hosea, I will marry you. All right, let me go and get my things, and then we will be on our way to your castle!" I drop his hand and turn towards the temple doors.

"No, please don't go back. And I don't have a castle." He suddenly doesn't sound so confident.

"I know you don't have a castle, it is just that when I was young… oh, never mind. Look, let me just get my stuff…"

"You don't need any reminder of who you were, Gomer. All things have been made new."

Since I don't know quite how to respond to that, I say the first thing that pops into my mind. "You do have a horse though, right? You have a horse, Hosea?"

"I have a donkey."

"Oh, donkeys are good too..."

## Chapter Five

# Newlywed

*"But I trust in your unfailing love; my heart rejoices in your salvation. I will sing to the Lord for he has been good to me."*
Psalm 13: 5&6

Oh, what a glorious day! It is so quiet in the early hours of the morning; I just love being the first one to make a sound. All creation seems to wait for me to speak before it comes alive. I love that! I close my eyes and breathe deeply. M-m-m-m... I smell the freshness of springtime, the fragrance of new beginnings in the air, and it's all so very...wonderful!

I have to laugh at myself. I used to hate people who were cheery and talkative early in the morning; I just wanted to slap them. But now I am all smiles and going on—so giddy, lately, that I want to slap myself. Seriously, it has been too long since I have seen a sunrise. Until recently, I saw only the darkness, for I rarely fell asleep before sunrise. I had forgotten how beautiful a sunrise could be.

The morning sky is just one small piece of beauty that Hosea brings into my life. Although we have only been married for a few months, it seems as though my former life never even existed—as though it had all been some kind of crazy, horrible nightmare.

25

Finally, I'm awake to my *real* life with Hosea, the life I was meant to live, the life I love.

I am so grateful to Hosea for all he has done for me. He took away all of my darkness, all of my sorrow. In their place are joy, light, love, and hope. Yes, hope for a future.

I used to dread the morning, the very thought of facing another day. Now I wake up smiling because I know he is there. For the first time since I was a little girl, I feel safe.

Really, the best part of being married to Hosea is the person I have become. I hated who I was; I couldn't even stand to look at myself. Now I realize that the beauty of his love is within me, and that is what makes me, well...beautiful. I mean, if Hosea loves me this much, I must be worth something, right?

The more time I spend with Hosea, the more I see how special he is. I care about him more with each passing day. That's why it kind of bothers me when I get certain thoughts in my head. For as far away as my former life seems, there are times when my past is right on my heels, nipping at me like some kind of rabid dog, ugly and vicious. Its saliva full of sin and death, its eyes reflect memories and lies; and I am terrified that it's coming to get me.

That is when I run. I run right to Hosea, and he helps me come to terms with the thoughts of my past. He holds me, he listens to me, and he never condemns me. Instead, he reminds me who I am now, and that I have nothing to fear, because he is with me no matter what.

Yet, at other times a memory of my past, comes to me more like... a cute little puppy dog, seemingly harmless and playful. I think to myself... *See, he's friendly. He won't hurt me. He just wants me to follow him and play. Just for a little while...nothing bad will happen.* And that is when I *don't* run to Hosea, when I want to go back—back to where I was when Hosea found me. Not permanently, like I said, just for a little while. True, it was a hard life, but…

I hear Hosea's footsteps.

"Good morning, my love." Hosea touches my hair and kisses my cheek.

"Good morning, husband." I say, returning his smile.

"You are up early again. Having some quiet time? I do not mean to intrude."

"No, please, sit. I have had quite a lot of quiet time since I have been here. Your home is very, very…peaceful." I hesitate because I seek the right word. I almost say, "Boring."

"I am glad you enjoy time to yourself, Gomer." Hosea moves closer to me and takes my hands.

"You are going away again, aren't you?" I ask with genuine disappointment.

"The Lord has given me a message for his people. A spirit of prostitution lives in their hearts. They make for themselves idols, they look to false gods. They trust in their own strength and in other nations. They have forgotten the Lord their God. They forget that it is He who gave them their strength, their power, their wealth." Hosea drops my hands and hangs his head. "I will be away longer this time, two weeks, maybe more."

"This burden is too much for you, Hosea. The people do not listen. You have done your part to warn them. Now, just stay with me and we can start our lives, start our family."

"Gomer…how I wish I could." Hosea rises to his feet and picks up his traveling bag.

"Hosea, when you leave me, I cannot help but feel you do not care about me. You love these people more than you love me."

"No, Gomer, I love God more than I love you, and for that you should be grateful. If it were not for the love of God..."

"If it were not for the love of God, what? Tell me, Hosea."

Hosea reaches for me and pulls me tight. He holds me for a long while then kisses the top of my head. With one last look back, he heads out the door, and I am once again, alone.

Alone.

Alone with thoughts of my past; good thoughts and bad thoughts all mixing together. The bad thoughts haunt me, beckon to me... and oddly it is the bad thoughts that make me want to go back...

All right, I will just go visit. I can be there and home before he even knows I am gone. Perhaps I can do a show or two. Just one of the chorus girls who wear the veils. No one will even know it is me. I miss the fun, the music, the thrill of the dance. I miss the applause and the attention.

I wonder who Yophe is with. I will cover my head and watch from afar. He will never even know I am there.

Strange. I sense that nagging little feeling again. The still, small voice that says, *"Don't. Don't do it..."*

I hear Hosea's voice, the day he asked me to marry him. *"No, please don't go back there. You don't need any reminders of who you were, Gomer. All things have been made new."*

Once again, anger wells up inside me. No one tells me what to do. It is my life and, married or not, I will make my own choices. He doesn't own me. No one owns me. I am free.

Believe me, I don't want to hurt Hosea. Not after all he has done for me. I would be a fool to throw away the beautiful life I have now.

And besides, what could possibly happen?

Chapter Six

# Mother of Three

*"...But one thing I do: Forgetting what is behind and straining
toward what is ahead."*
Phillipians 3:13

I wonder what hour it is. The baby is finally sleeping, so this is my
only chance to rest, for I fear the sun will rise soon.

But I am awake. I have trouble sleeping lately, so when the day
comes, I am tired—very, very tired. Demons of my past haunt me
in the still dark hours before dawn, when I cannot sleep. I try to
put thoughts of my past out of my mind, but lately I am losing the
battle to keep them away.

I remember years ago, when Hosea and I were first married, I
thought I could go visit a few friends at the temple. How foolish,
thinking I could go back to my old neighborhood and not be
affected by it. I cannot believe how quickly I became my old self.
I guess I still *was* my old self. When I fell into that same old sin, I
thought about staying there and accepting the fact that all I would
ever be is a shameful prostitute. But somehow, even through the
ugliness of my sin, I had the most incredible sense of Hosea's love
for me and, looking back now, I see how his love drew me home.

31

Of course, when I went back, I tried to pretend that nothing ever happened, but he knew. Somehow, he knew, and I hated him for that. Truthfully, I hated myself for not telling him. My secret put such distance between us that the guilt was suffocating me. Pretending to be something you're not is a horrible way to live.

Just when I thought things couldn't get any worse, I realized I was pregnant. Something I had longed for all my life was happening, but because of my sin, the joy of that event was taken from me.

Oh, I remember how much I wanted to be sure the baby was Hosea's, but I could not be sure. I was sure of one thing, though. I could not live another day without telling him. I played the scene over and over in my head, trying to imagine his reaction. I knew he had every right to hate me and cast me out like a dog in the street. Part of me actually wanted him to because, in my heart, I knew the street was where I belonged.

With much fear, I confessed. Hosea was quiet for long while, and I sat there, holding my breath, waiting for my husband to pronounce judgment. I knew that, under the law, I deserved death.

After what seemed like an eternity, Hosea knelt down and touched my face. Wiping my tears away, he whispered, "I have loved you with an everlasting love. I have drawn you with loving kindness. I have betrothed you to me forever. I have betrothed you in righteousness and justice, and in love and compassion. You are forgiven."

As my family sleeps, in the predawn darkness I remember his words as though it were yesterday, and I recall the joy I felt when Hosea forgave me. I remember saying to him, "Thank you, Hosea. Thank you for loving me. Thank you for forgiving me. I promise I will never hurt you again. I will never, never hurt you…"

Those words trigger another memory, a darker one, for I ended up saying those words to Hosea over and over again, "I will never,

never..." And yet I hurt him again and again. I don't even know why I kept going back to my sin. Was it habit? Was it ignorance? Was it selfishness? I guess I didn't understand how much I was hurting him, and I definitely didn't understand how much he loved me. Then one day it hit me—he did love me. He loved me. HE... LOVED...ME.

So I find myself wanting to be worthy of the love this man has for me. Many, many years have passed since I last strayed away, so I guess I have finally changed! Yes, yes, think about the good things, Gomer. Hold on to the good thoughts.

I think I changed...

I wish I could sleep right now. That would be a good change.

Changes... Motherhood sure can change a woman. Years ago, when I had my first child, I had a hard time. All the other mothers I knew were happy and content with their lives, and I...well, I wasn't. Happiness eluded me.

I had spent years building walls to protect my heart from being hurt, and I feared that the barrier would not allow me to love my child as I should. However, as I cared for this precious infant, tenderness and warmth grew day by day. The walls crumbled, and I loved him. I loved him dearly.

Now, many years and three kids later, it still terrifies me to love this much because, I know, looking at each precious little innocent face, that the only way anyone will ever hurt me again is to hurt this child. I will never let anyone hurt my children. I know I may not be able to shelter them forever, but I vowed to myself and to God above that none of them would ever know the kind of life I had lived. They will never suffer in sin the way I suffered in sin. They will not follow in my footsteps. No, they will follow in the path of righteousness the way their father has...I mean, the way Hosea has.

I love watching Hosea with the kids. He couldn't love them more if they were…

Well, the point is, I just don't want them to turn out like me.

## Chapter Seven

# I am Nothing

*"But Godliness with contentment is great gain."*
I Timothy 6:6

The sun is almost up and there is so much to do. It seems as though, no matter how early I start, the day is never long enough. I get up earlier and earlier just to get some things done before the kids awake.

*I feel so angry.*

Hey, here is an idea—why don't I just try not going to bed at all, huh? Would that work for everyone?

I'm sorry. It sounds as though I'm complaining, and I don't mean to complain. After all, this is what I wanted for my life, right? To become a wife and mother. They say that watching my children grow and be happy and healthy, well, that should be enough thanks for all I do. It isn't.

*No one appreciates me.*

Oh, here's a good one. Children are a reward from the Lord, which just rewards me with more work, which makes me just want to scream sometimes! What about me, huh? What about a little time for myself? All day long I have duties and responsibilities and people pulling at me, "Mommy! Mommy..." and I never get to do what I want to do. I never get to go where I want to go. It's as though no one even sees me anymore.

*I am invisible.*

I need...something. I need to feel appreciated. Would it kill anyone to say thank you once in a while? I guess they appreciate me when I feed them, but is it enough? God knows I want it to be enough. I don't know what to do anymore.

My life needs meaning and purpose.

Don't get me wrong, Hosea is a great husband, but it was different in the beginning.

*I got more attention when I strayed away.*

I used to be pretty. Did you know that? At one time I had sparkly jewelry and beautiful clothes. It may be hard to picture this now, but there was a time when I could turn a lot of heads.

*But look at me now.*

I don't know what to do to feel happy anymore.

*God help me, I don't know anything anymore.*

Startled out of my thoughts by the baby's cry, I feel an overwhelming urge to run. *Just leave, no one will care.* I am torn between comforting my child and walking away.

I feel nothing. As though in a dream, outside of myself, I walk out the door and down the darkened street, not knowing where I am going. I do not have a cloak, but I don't care.

Suddenly, a figure in the shadows near the olive trees calls out to me, but I can barely hear him. What did he say? Again, a raspy whisper in the wind, "I've been waiting for you." *Who are you?* My thoughts are jumbled. Nothing makes sense...

The figure is in front of me, blocking me, reaching for me. "I never forgot you, Gomer. I have been waiting for you to come to me. Don't you want to feel pretty again, Gomer?"

He leads me behind the stone wall. He touches me, but I feel nothing.

*I am nothing.*

## Chapter Eight

# Unclean

*"Be self-controlled and alert. Your enemy the devil prowls around
like a roaring lion looking for someone to devour."*
I Peter 5:8

Oh, what have I done? I said I would never do it again. I
promised. I promised myself. I promised my husband that I would
be faithful, that I would change. And I thought I had. I thought I
had changed.

I would give anything to take back what I've done to Hosea!
After all he has done for me—the love he has given me. He
believed in me, and now I have gone and thrown it all away by
hurting him once again.

Please, God, please, you have to help me! Please roll back the
days and give me another chance. Please, just one more chance.

But I have used up all my chances.

What is wrong with me? I can't keep doing this. It was one thing
when I didn't know any better, and time and time again he took me
back. Yes, he forgave me over and over again when I was younger.
But not now, not this time. Not after all these years that I have
known him, and lived with him, and loved him...or at least

pretended to love him, for how could I love him and sin against him at the same time? I have wiped away our entire future.

This time, I knew what I was doing. I knew what the consequences would be and I chose. *I* chose! *I chose*!

It's time to face who I really am. The changes I thought I had made in my life were all lies. Hosea had me believing that I could truly change—a nice dream, but that is all it was. The truth is I am what I am. A hypocrite. A big fake. I can no longer pretend to be a godly woman when I know the evil that lies in my heart.

Hosea, you deserve so much better. You deserve a godly woman, and now I know I can never be that for you. I have broken my marriage vows, and I can never make it right again; but one vow I intend to keep, even if it means my death.

I make my way back to my house and stand before the open window of the room where my children are asleep. In the suffocating silence of my sin, my heart silently speaks to them: "My precious children, I promised that I would always love you, and always protect you. I hope you know that what I do now, I do out of love, and that I am protecting you. I'm protecting you from…me. Mommy wanted to be so much for you, but all I seem to do is hurt the people that I love, so I have to go away for fear that you will turn out like me. I want you to know, though no matter where I go or the distance between us, I will always be your mother."

As I press my forehead against the cold stone frame of the window, tears roll down my cheeks and fall to the dust below. I whisper a barely audible prayer that I know no one will hear, "Forgive me. Please, find it in your hearts to forgive me."

Yet, wiping my tears with the back of my hand, I know there is no more forgiveness. Not for me. Not this time. I linger by the window. I want to run inside and tell them all I'm sorry. I want to kiss my babies. I want to hold them and never let go.

But nothing unclean will ever touch my children, so I turn and walk away.

## Chapter Nine

# The Auction Block

*"I have seen his ways and I will heal him; I will guide him and restore him."* Isaiah 57:18

"Go on, go on...get out there. Get out there!" The man who bound my hands pushes me. I cannot see where I am. My eyes are swollen and what's left of my hair is matted and hanging in my face. Men with brutal hands and calloused hearts grab at me and drag me in front of the crowd. I listen to the bidding for the people in front of me, two of whom are children. Men and women, young and old; we are all in chains. *How did they come to be here?*

All I wanted was to feel pretty again. I thought I could go back—but they mocked me. I wanted to dance, just one more time. But they laughed at me. Yophe said, "Sure, you can be part of the show." So he put a feed bag over my head...and...

It is my turn. I am shoved forward. Someone shouts, "Look at that sorry wretch. You couldn't even *give* her away!"

He is right. No one will want me. The laughter, the insults, they mean nothing to me, for I am already dead. Sin has brought me to this place. It is sin that chains me to this auction block, and sin is stealing my life away.

In these final moments, I have clear thought, and one realization.

In all the years I knew Hosea, all I ever cared about was what he could do for me. If ever my selfish needs were not met, I strayed away. I loved him only when he made me feel good about myself. Now that we are separated forever, I finally realize it was never about what he could do, but only about who he was. I couldn't even see who he was until I got myself out of the way.

Now I see him—his gentleness, his kindness, his beauty.

I miss him. How I long to see him just one more time—feel his touch, see his smile. If I could say just one thing, I would say... I'm sorry. I am so, so sorry.

I love him because he is worthy and deserving of all my love. Hosea gave me a new, respectable life, and sin has stolen that life away. As a result of my own choices, I am here on this auction block, mocked and spit on by the crowd. In my ears the auctioneer shouts, "Who will start the bidding for this broken, dirty wretch?" The only answer is laughter from the crowd.

It seems an eternity until a voice calls from the distance, "Fifteen pieces of silver."

The voice, however faint, sends a glimmer of hope into my heart, for *I know that voice.*

Again, I hear, "Fifteen pieces of silver."

The voice grows stronger, getting closer. Suddenly the crowd parts...

*Is that you?*

Then the voice declares, "Fifteen pieces of silver is far too small a price for...for my beautiful wife. I would buy her with my life."

Suddenly, the chains that bind my hands and heart are loosed forever and, for the first time in my life, his words make sense to me! I finally realize I am his beautiful wife. I am a pure and spotless bride. Not because of anything I could ever do, but only because of his incredible redeeming love can I ever be forgiven. I am completely forgiven! I know the truth is, when I look into his eyes, that nothing I do would ever make him stop loving me. He searched for me, he found me, and he bought me back. He never gave up on me.

Hosea takes a soft cloth and wipes my face. Gently, he whispers in my ear, "I have come for you."

I can barely get the words out, "You knew all along, didn't you? You knew the whole time that one day I would love you. You knew one day I would truly be yours. Take me home. I want to go home. Thank you, God, that I still have a home."

Hosea picks me up in his arms and carries me through the crowd.

## Chapter Ten

# Not Home Yet

*"I will betroth you to me forever; I will betroth you to me in righteousness and justice, in love and compassion. I will betroth you in faithfulness, and you will acknowledge the Lord."*
Hosea 2:19-20

We do not speak as we travel in the direction of our home. To my surprise, though, we don't go home. Instead, Hosea takes me to a tiny stone house on the other side of our village. He carries me through the doorway and sets me down on a mat in the main living area. I notice the house is clean and looks comfortable, though quite empty, save for a pallet for a bed, linens, jugs, a few cups and bowls, and some dried fruit.

"Where am I?" My voice is cracked and hoarse.

"You are in a rented house. My father is paying for it."

"Where are the children?" I fight back tears. "I thought everything was going to be all right, that we would just go back to being a family."

"I have arranged for them to stay with Josiah and his family. I think it best if they do not see you for a while." Hosea busies himself pouring a cup of water and gathering a blanket for me.

"Of course, you are right. I would only frighten them." I wonder what I must look like, a strange and swollen monster.

"You must heal. Lydia will care for you." Hosea wipes my brow with a cool cloth.

"And you, where will you be?" I stop his hand.

Without a word, Hosea rises and places the cloth into the basin. Returning to my bedside, he is tender, but firm. "You are to stay with me many days. You must not play the harlot. You shall not have any man. Not even me."

"I don't understand." My heart sinks. "You said I should stay with you, but I am not staying with you." The tears come, first one or two; then I break into sobs. I cry so hard that I think perhaps the rest of my ribs will break. Hosea holds me but doesn't say anything. Soon he releases his embrace and stands to his feet.

"You must heal." He walks out the door.

Too weak to stand, I cannot go after him. I am alone and, for the first time in my life, I begin to pray from my heart.

*Lord God, the mercy you have shown me through Hosea is more than I deserve. I should be dead right now. With all the commotion, I forgot to tell Hosea that I am sorry. But I realize that I should be telling You that I'm sorry. I am truly sorry for what I have done. The love Hosea shows, it has to be from You. No man would be able to do this on his own—speak to people who do not listen, love a woman who does not love in return. This is far greater love than man is capable of.*

*You are the one true God. I guess I have always known You were real; I just didn't want to stop sinning. I didn't want to listen. I see, now, where my choices have gotten me.*

*Please, Lord, help me get my children back. I don't know why I have to stay in this place. I told you that I am truly sorry. Please, God, help me get home. I just want to go home...*

The days and weeks pass. Lydia, a woman from our village, tends to me. She bathes me, feeds me, but she never speaks. I try to talk to her, but I soon give up. I wonder if Hosea has instructed her not to talk to me. I feel as though I am being punished.

He comes to me. Every day, Hosea comes to me, and he reads from a scroll. He does not speak his own words. He comes, sits by my bedside, and reads from the scroll for a few minutes, sometimes longer. Then he just folds the scroll and leaves.

I have come to realize the scroll is God's Word, and Hosea is starting at the beginning. At first, I carry too much anger to even listen, and I have to quiet the voices in my head. *Why have you put me here? Why do you not speak to me? Why are you punishing me?*

I resent having to stay in this lonely house all by myself. I resent his silence. And I resent the fact that he does not tell me that he loves me. Somehow, though, the words he reads from the scroll eventually take root in my heart, and, like an ember in the breeze, they begin to glow. An inner warmth fills my being, and I am overcome with an amazing sense of...peace.

Days pass.

I wait for his daily visit. With a smile, I remember the first time Hosea ever read to me. "'In the beginning, God created the heavens and the earth. Now the earth was formless and empty, darkness was over the surface of the deep, and the Spirit of God was hovering over the waters. And God said, "Let there be light," and there was light.'"

Now that my anger has subsided, I find myself looking forward to his visits. What will Hosea read today? Every day, as my body heals, my heart heals as well. My spirit is alive. The zeal in my heart that started as a small ember, fans into flame more every day as I hear the Word of the Lord.

Today I hear footsteps nearing my door. Thinking it is Hosea, I ready myself for his reading. But instead of his familiar voice announcing his arrival, I hear the voice of a child, and then another, and then one more.

My children!

Oh, the joy of our reunion! They run to me and dive into my lap. Thankfully, I have healed enough to enjoy three children jumping on me and hugging me all at once. Tears and laughter all mix together, and they ask a million questions I cannot possibly answer. *Oh, God, thank You, thank You!*

I hold each one, and drink in the smell of their hair. I touch their faces, tracing the shapes of their noses and lips. I straighten their clothing. I want to brush my daughter's hair. I want to hold my youngest like a baby, although he isn't a baby anymore.

"I love you..." I feel as though I will burst.

"We love you, Mommy. Oh, Mommy..." My youngest buries his head in my tunic. We cry together.

"Well, let me look at you. You have all grown so much." How long has it been? I don't even know.

The first visit with the children is short. Hosea arrives and takes them away after what seems to be only a few minutes. I want to follow, but I have promised to do whatever he wants me to do to get my family back, and that means staying in this house until he decides I am ready. Though difficult, I must allow myself to be humbled in such a way. I am determined not to mess this up—not this time.

Time passes.

Today, I receive a surprise. My beautiful daughter comes by herself to visit me—so grown up! She reminds me a great deal of Hosea—mature, yet playful in nature, and wise beyond her years.

"Mother," she begins, "We have been learning about the Hebrew wedding traditions. They are very beautiful."

"My daughter, are you trying to tell me something? You are too young! Is your father trying to marry you off already?"

"No mother! He is not. Some of us girls are learning the Hebrew practices of the betrothal ceremony. Father says that marriage is an expression of God's love for us, and the beautiful ceremony speaks of God's promise of a coming savior."

"Yes, I remember learning about God's promise of a Savior when your father read the scroll to me."

"Yes! He reads the scroll to us, as well, every day. Anyway, mother, the first thing that happens when a couple gets engaged is that the young man gives a cup of wine to the girl he is going to marry. Well, he doesn't just give it to her, she has to take it. It is called the cup of acceptance."

"What if she doesn't want to marry the boy?" I ask. I really did want to know.

"Well, she has the right of refusal. But he probably really hopes she doesn't refuse him."

"Yes, I am sure. So if she accepts, is it legally binding—like a covenant, a promise?"

"Yes, and then the young man goes and prepares a place for them to live when they get married. And the groom's father helps his son build the house, or the room, or whatever. It is actually the father who tells the son when he can go get his bride."

"When he feels the house is ready?" I ask.

"Uh-huh," she says, nodding her head. She continues in earnest, "Now, when the groom is away preparing a place for them to live, the bride has to get her wedding garments ready. She has to keep them neat and clean, careful not to wrinkle her beautiful dress, for she never knows when her groom will come for her."

"I see." There is sadness in my voice, but thankfully my sweet daughter does not notice.

"Mother, this is the best part. The bridegroom's father gives the command, and the wedding processional starts! The groom gathers his friends, and they march through the streets carrying oil lamps. They blow a shofar, mother. You know, the ram's horn trumpet. They come to the bride's home, and she is carried away with her groom to a joyous wedding celebration! Oh, mother, can you just imagine?"

I cannot speak.

"Mother? Are you all right?"

"I'm tired now, Dear."

"Of course, all my talking has worn you out. I'm sorry."

"Nothing to be sorry about. Please give the other children a kiss for me. Your father, too." I dissolve into tears as she walks out the door.

It stabs my heart that the children no longer ask when I am coming home.

This is the life we have all come to accept. I mourn the things that will never be, and the loss of dreams that will never come to pass. I once thought that we would be a family again, that everything would be put back together, but I have to lay my desires down. I have to let go.

*God, I give my life and my future to you. I give you my dreams. I know I have messed my life up, and I am living with the consequences of my actions. This beautiful wedding ceremony my daughter speaks of. This is something I will never have. But, please Lord, let my daughter know this joy. Please do not let her make the same mistakes I have made. Hosea will choose well for her; he will find her a good man. May she experience the life I can only dream of.*

As each day passes, Hosea's voice grows sweeter and tenderer. Yesterday, he touched my hand as he read from the scroll. I thought my heart would leap out of my chest. I must admit, I have never been attracted to him until now. His profile is so handsome. I love the shape of his nose. A desire stirs within me, from the moment I hear his footsteps. I dream about him…

He should be here soon. I feel like a young girl with a crush, and I get butterflies in my stomach waiting for him to come visit me. I melt at the sound of his voice and dream of the day he kisses me.

I hear him! Today he enters with a big smile.

"We will read from the first section of the book of Moses. Do you know why I read to you often from the first book, from Genesis?" he asks me, laying the scroll at his feet.

"No Hosea, I do not know."

"Because God's Word is truth from the very first verse. Genesis is the foundation of our faith. If the first part isn't true, then none of it is true. Do you understand, Gomer?"

"Yes, I understand. I believe it all, Hosea. I trust and believe every word of the Holy Scriptures. It has…it has changed me." I am excited to have a real conversation with Hosea. For so long, he only spoke God's writings to me. As thrilling as it was to hear God's Word, a different kind of excitement overtakes me as I hear Hosea's words. Just think, there was a time when I didn't want Hosea to talk to me.

"I can see the Word of God has changed you, Gomer."

"I am so glad you notice a difference in me; but I must ask you, Hosea, why have you not spoken to me? For all these months, why have you only read from the scroll? Were you punishing me?"

"No, I did not mean my actions to appear as punishment. The Word of God is not punishment. It is life and liberty, and the only force powerful enough to change the human heart."

I draw closer to him. "I sense, perhaps, there is another reason?"

Hosea sighs and takes my hand. "You had become my idol, Gomer. I preached to everyone else, without realizing that I myself was guilty of idolatry by putting you first in my heart, above God. For all the years you lived with me, I tried to win you with *my* words. I tried to change you with my great knowledge of God. I thought I could save you and make you righteous in my own strength, in my own power. I was wrong."

"I'm sorry, what did you say?" A smile creeps across my face.

"You heard me." Hosea reaches down to fidget with his sandal, but I know he is trying to hide his own smile.

"No, I'm quite sure I did not, because I thought I heard you say that you were wrong, and the Hosea I know would never say such a thing. Hosea is never wrong, and he never makes mistakes."

"God humbled me while you were gone, Gomer."

"Glad I'm not the only one."

"When we were first married, God was first in my life; but over the years, I let thoughts of you consume me. My love is not perfect, Gomer; only God's love is perfect. I'm a man who makes mistakes, just like anyone else. When the Word of the Lord came to me, and I began to prophesy to the people, I thought I was above everyone. I guess I let the power of my ministry go to my head, and I'm sorry for the times my prideful arrogance made you feel unworthy."

"Just hearing you admit you were wrong about something makes all my pain and suffering worthwhile!" I take my hand away and playfully hit him on the arm.

"I deserve much worse than a slap on the arm." Hosea kicks back and laughs, really laughs. I can't remember the last time I heard him laugh like that. "I even had little Gomer idol statues made, and I had to smash them all in repentance."

"Oh, stop it!" I hit him again, harder, and we both laugh for a long while, until we can't laugh anymore. Then there is a long silence as we collect ourselves.

"Well," he wipes the tears of laughter from his eyes, "we will now have our reading from the Word of the Lord."

"Shouldn't you pick the scroll up first?" I ask.

"I have this part memorized. I want to look at you as I speak."

"Why?"

"Because I like to look at you."

I roll my eyes.

He takes a moment and then, in an almost heavenly voice, he recites the account of Adam and Eve. Although he has read it before, this time the words encircle my heart like a warm embrace. "'So the Lord God caused the man to fall into a deep sleep; and while he was sleeping, he took one of the man's ribs and closed up the place with flesh. Then the Lord God made a woman from the rib he had taken out of man, and he brought her to the man. The man said, "This is now bone of my bones and flesh of my flesh... and they will become one flesh.'"

A holy presence fills the room. Neither wants to disturb the beauty of this moment, so we sit hand in hand and look for answers in each other's eyes. Apparently Hosea has his answer. A look of relief, then pure joy crosses his face, and he grins at me.

"I have to go," is all he says, and he walks out the door.

What? He just walks out? That's it? I thought for sure that this would be the day that he would say I can come home! ...Maybe it's true ...maybe I'll never go home. Maybe this really is my life. I've feared it before, but now I know for sure—this is my life.

*God, please help me. Please help me accept my life. Even if nothing changes, I have to praise You; I have to keep drawing strength from Your Word. I can do this if I know You are with me. I release Hosea to You, I release my marriage to You...I release my children. Amen.*

Utterly alone, I cry myself to sleep.

## Chapter Eleven

# The Bridegroom Comes

*"The bride belongs to the bridegroom. The friend who attends the bridegroom waits and listens for him, and is full of joy when he hears the bridegroom's voice."*
John 3:29

Around midnight, I am awakened by a commotion down the street. Startled at first, I am afraid to move, afraid that someone will know I am here alone. I lie still and listen. The voices are faint, but I can tell that many people are quickly approaching. Perhaps an angry mob...no, wait. The voices sound happy and excited. And is that music that I hear? What kind of celebration can possibly be going on at this time of night?

And then I hear it—the shofar!

Everything my daughter had told me about the wedding traditions comes flooding into my mind. In the darkness of my tiny room, I sit up and rub my eyes, still swollen from my tears. I smile to myself as I picture a confident and joyful groom triumphantly coming for his bride! Oh, how beautiful her garments must be— fine linen, bright and clean, and flowers for her hair. I can only imagine the bountiful marriage banquet that awaits them. Surely, there is a wonderful home awaiting the beautiful bride, one that her bridegroom has lovingly prepared for her.

*Whoever this is, Lord, bless them.*

I drink in the music and the laughter and, in my mind, I join the happy procession. Expecting them to pass by, I prepare myself to accept the emptiness that will surely envelop me when I can no longer hear their celebration. Instead, they stop outside my door.

Suddenly, the door opens, and I spring to my feet. One by one, an entourage of women files in, led by my own dear daughter. She carries a gorgeous white dress, made of the finest linen. Behind her, a woman carries a veil, and another, a beautiful array of flowers. Several others carry oil lamps; and crowd into my tiny house.

"Honey, you are so young!" I say to my daughter. "I thought you said your father was not ready to marry you off."

All the ladies look at one another and giggle.

"No, Momma." My daughter holds the dress out to me. "This is for you."

Feeling as though I might faint, I take a step backward and lean against the stone wall, both hands to my mouth. I look first to the dress, then to my daughter's face, then back to the dress. Then I notice the warm smile on the face of each woman there. They don't even know me, but their love fills the room.

"How can this be?" Too shocked for words, I stand there, afraid it is all a dream.

"You don't want to keep your groom waiting…" The lady who holds the flowers nods her head towards the door.

"My groom?" I manage to collect my strength, walk to the window, and peer out into the street. There I behold the most beautiful sight I have ever seen. Hosea's face is lit by the glow of his lamp, and he has never been more handsome. The lamps of the others line the street.

"I have come for you." Hosea lets out a shout of joy and raises his lamp, and all the others shout in response and lift their lamps to the heavens.

The ladies pull me inside, dress me in the fine, clean linen, adorn my hair with flowers, and drape the veil over my head and face. I cannot stop crying, but these are tears of joy.

"You look beautiful, Momma." My daughter smooths my dress and opens the door for me. The women chime in, "Lovely...yes, lovely."

Everyone cheers when I appear in the doorway. They applaud as Hosea takes my hands, and we stand face to face. Hosea lifts my veil and kisses me. It has been so long... so long that it feels like...a first kiss.

Everything has been made new.

We begin to walk through the lamplit street, and with each step the applause grows louder. Amidst the laughter and the cheers, I hear another sound. Soft at first, like the gentleness of a dove. The sound swirls around and engulfs my spirit in a passionate embrace. Love envelops me, and then I hear it loud and clear—a new song...a love song. My groom rejoices over me with singing, and I realize where the light is leading me...

I'm going home.

# Part 2

# Geri's Story

~

Chapter Twelve

# Ther♀ is ♀lways a Way Back Home

*"But by the grace of God I am what I am..."*
1 Corinthians 15:10 a

My name is Geri. I know, strange name for a girl. My given name is Geraldine but no one calls me that except my mother and my third grade teacher, Mrs. Sherman. My name means "ruler with a spear" and, if you ask my husband and kids, it is a very fitting name for me. One time I saw a plaque that defined the name *Geraldine* as "victorious one." I liked that description better. The plaque now hangs in my kitchen. Victorious one! I love that because, you see, I was not always victorious. Defeated one, unworthy one, self-absorbed one, fearful one, yes. But certainly not "victorious one."

As a child, I loved the Lord. I gave my heart to Jesus as a young teenager. Something was always missing, though. My parents divorced when I was sixteen, but the trouble started before that. Dad had a drinking problem, and I always felt bad for him. He truly loved my mother, and it broke my heart that she didn't seem to love him. Because mom didn't show love to my father, I didn't either. For years, I pretended he wasn't even there. Looking back, I can see how this formed a gaping hole in my life.

I was a fixer. I wanted to fix everything. I wanted to fix my parents' marriage; I wanted to fix my father. I wanted him to have love in his life. Of course, I couldn't fix anything, but I sure tried, only not in the way one would think.

I have a childhood memory of my mother ironing my father's shirts. Even if they'd had a horrible fight the night before, I took comfort in hearing my mom get up in the morning, take out the ironing board, and iron my dad's shirt. It was my way of knowing she still loved him, despite her inability to show it. It was my sign that everything was going to be all right.

One chilly morning, I heard the familiar sound of the squeaky ironing board. I got out of bed to ready myself for school and went to the kitchen to say good morning to my mother. Instead of my mom, I saw my dad in the kitchen, fumbling with the iron and the board, trying to get his shirt laid out right. He apparently didn't know how to iron.

It was so cold in the kitchen. It was so cold in my house. My mother never ironed his shirt again.

Why do I mention this story? In Bible College, at 21 years of age, I met a man who reminded me very much of my father. I tried to bring closure to an extremely painful part of my life by involving myself with this man. When we started dating, I offered to iron his shirts. Men were not allowed in the girl's dorms so, after bringing me his shirts, he sat in the outer lobby, and I happily ironed inside. Yes, I was going to fix everything by marrying this man, even though we barely knew each other. Thus began the downward spiral of my life.

Having grown up in a home with parents who constantly fought, I didn't know what real love between a man and woman was supposed to look like. I viewed a volatile and harmful relationship as normal, so I couldn't recognize that the young man I married was very troubled. I had no idea that he didn't love me, because I didn't know that love wasn't supposed to tear down and destroy; and I didn't understand why I couldn't fix things.

In our first year of marriage, my husband dropped out of Bible College and began to reveal his true nature. He was unfaithful to me, and intentionally used it to destroy me. We ended up divorced, and it broke my heart. All my dreams, everything I ever wanted, were being stripped away from me. It wasn't fair!

I blamed God. I just wanted to shout at Him.

*How could You do this to me? I am about to graduate from Bible college. There is no way I can go into ministry now. Where are You, God? Obviously, You don't care about me, or You would never have let this happen. Well, if You don't care about me, then I don't care about You! I'm done.*

I walked away from God, from church, and from any thought of ever serving Him. I stopped reading my Bible and listening to Christian music. I stopped hanging out with my Christian friends. I tried to stop any thoughts of the Lord from entering my mind, and I know I tried to stop loving Him. I can even go so far as to say that I endeavored to hurt Jesus.

You see, through it all, I knew deep down that He loved me. Jesus Christ loved me, so I wanted to hurt Him by giving myself to His enemy, Satan. I went to bars, got into relationships that I should not have been in, and I pretended I was happy. I ran from God for seven years.

After one particularly evil day of my life, I sat alone in my bedroom. I could actually feel the heaviness of the chains of sin wrapping around my heart and mind. Suddenly, something broke through the ugliness of the evil that engulfed me.

*Love.*

I felt the presence of love—real and powerful—and the weight lifted, as the presence of Jesus Christ filled my room. His presence was love like none I had never known. I remember saying out loud, "Please Lord, You shouldn't be here. Don't You know what I have become? Maybe once I could have loved You. Maybe once I could have served You—when I was a good girl in Bible college, but not now. Please leave me..."

Never before and never since has this happened to me, but I truly felt the arms of my Savior wrap around me and hold me. Instead of leaving, the love of Jesus grew stronger and stronger, and not in an audible voice, but in my heart, I heard the words, "You are my beautiful bride."

*How can you still call me that?* The words echoed in my mind.

Still, Jesus just held me, and I came face to face with Christ's redeeming love. He held me until I melted at the side of my bed in a pool of tears.

"Lord, if You'll take me back, I promise to use my gifts and talents to tell others that there is always a way back home to You."

I rededicated my life to God that night, and He began a healing process in me that lasted a long time. I spent a lot of time alone with the Lord over the next couple of years, learning His Word and getting to know Him better. I began what I call "The Divine Romance" with Jesus. In order to break away from a relationship with a man who had a very strong hold on me, I moved out of state to a place where I hardly knew anyone. Although sometimes I did feel quite lonely, Jesus revealed His love to me during my times of solitude, teaching me what God's love looks like—beautiful, pure, kind, trustworthy, patient, and selfless.

Without the "Divine Romance" experience with Jesus, I never would have been able to recognize a Christ-like character in a man, let alone have been attracted to those qualities. When my mind and heart healed enough to finally understand what a Godly man looked like, and to appreciate the value of such a man, the Lord brought Rich Campbell, also a Bible college graduate, into my life. Little did I know that God had moved him out of his home state, too, and that, before we met, we had lived in apartments that overlooked each other for a whole year.

Rich and I married on Christmas Eve, 1999. A year later, a beautiful daughter arrived. When Rich asked me what girl names I liked, I said, "Mercy." I wanted to name her after the one word that summed up my walk with God. Two and half years later, the Lord gave us a son whom we named Christopher.

God has greatly blessed us. Life changed and, although being married and raising two kids kept us very busy, Rich and I began to pray for the Lord to show us the best way to serve Him. I remembered my promise to God that I would use my gifts and talents to tell people about Him. I waited for the Holy Spirit to show me what to do, because I felt that once-dying desire to serve God come more alive in my heart every day.

One morning at church, I heard God whisper in my ear, "Tell them I love them…" From that moment on, the call of God gripped my heart. Having been on stage all of my life, I knew the best way to tell people that God loved them was to incorporate my story, or my testimony into a stage production, drawing from an article I had read years earlier about the Biblical account of Gomer and Hosea.

This true story in the Word of God told of Gomer, a sinful woman who had to be forgiven time after time. I thought, *That's me!* I read about her faithful husband, Hosea, who loved her no matter what she did, and he never gave up on her. I thought, *That's Jesus!* The message of Gomer and Hosea inspired me to write the script of a stage play titled *The Story of Gomer.* Every day for almost a year, I sat in my car during my lunch hour, praying for God to give me the right words that would tell the story of this inspiring couple. I prayed that the Lord would show me His heart.

That script turned into a one woman, one hour stage play. I presented the play for the first time at my home church in 2004, and I had fourteen bookings in the first year. *The Story of Gomer* has now been performed in more than 150 churches and organizations, and the script is presently being translated into its third language.

My heartfelt desire is that, by sharing my story, I might help you to know you are loved. If you come to Christ in true repentance of your sin, you are forgiven. No matter where you have been or what you have done, there is a God who loves you, a Savior that pursues you. He will never stop longing for you.

If there were just one thing God could say to you, just one sentence that you could hear, I truly believe it would be, "I love you."

My prayer for you, dear reader, is that one day not only will you be able to hear God speak these words into your heart, but that you will also believe it. If your commitment to Him is real, He will change your life!

## Chapter Thirteen

# Second Chance

*"For he has rescued us from the dominion of darkness and brought us into the kingdom of the Son he loves, in whom we have redemption, the forgiveness of sins."*
Colossians 1:13, 14

In 2003, my father suffered a brain aneurism and almost died. I got a call with the grave news, "Get on a plane as quick as you can, your father may not make it through the night." I flew to Syracuse on the next available flight, praying that God would intervene. *Please, God, don't let him die.* My father was now happily remarried, and he and I had developed a very close relationship. Still, I knew he had not made his peace with God.

My dad was many years removed from the violent alcoholic who almost put his fist through the wall when I said I had given my heart to the Lord and wanted to go to church with my girlfriend's family. He remained hostile towards God and the idea that, if he didn't receive Christ as Savior, he would spend eternity apart from God. He had a lot of trouble seeing himself as a "sinner" in need of anything. In fact, before Rich and I got married, he told my husband-to-be, "You keep your religion to yourself, and we'll get along just fine." When Rich and I first started our ministry, it broke my heart that my dad really didn't want to hear about what I was doing to serve God. He liked that I was on stage. He even came to see my play *The Story of Gomer*, but he never wanted to talk about the message of the play, or about how we were impacting lives for Christ.

I pondered these thoughts as I sat holding his unresponsive hand, listening to him breathe with the machines and wires hooked up to his body. I prayed, and I sang to him. I had no idea if he could hear me. *Lord, you are the God of second chances; please give my father a second chance.*

Dad remained in a coma for many days. I stayed as long as I could but, eventually, I had to return home to my 2-year old daughter. I was not able to be present, when, miraculously, my father woke up. I thanked God and looked forward to hearing updates from my stepmother as she me kept informed on his progress.

Very few people heal from a brain aneurism as well as my dad did; his recovery was nothing short of a miracle. He learned to do everything all over again, and spent many months in rehab. When he was finally able to write again, he sent me cards and letters. In his letters were the words, "Thank you for bringing people closer to God. Keep doing what you're doing. You make me very happy." In another, "Please continue your life as you have, doing good and getting rid of the bad things, introducing people to good things and leading them to heaven." It was hard for him to put thoughts together, and his letters may have been worded a little funny, but Rich and I could tell beyond any doubt that these were the words of a changed man.

Some may attribute my father's change to the brain injury, and some may think his words about God did not make sense, but they made perfect sense to me. When we were finally able to visit together, I absolutely saw and sensed a deep spiritual change in my father.

He told me an incredible account of his coma experience. I had heard and read about people with near-death experiences, but I had never known any such person. I must admit that I wasn't sure I believed any of it. But the conviction in my father's voice and the tears that he shed as he told me what happened are forever imprinted in my memory.

"I died," my father began, "and I felt as though I went to heaven, but God wouldn't let me in. It's as if I heard Him say 'You have to go back, you cannot come in.'" That experience forever changed him. When he came out of his coma, he came out a believer in Christ.

Three years later, in 2006, I visited my dad at his camp in Alexandria Bay. Sitting at a picnic table by the St. Lawrence River, I asked him if he would like to be absolutely sure that he would go to heaven. We talked of salvation, not by works, but by faith in God and in His Son Jesus. We talked of repentance and second chances. We talked about the sacrifice of Jesus and his death on the cross for our sins. Then, with my husband alongside me, I led my dad in a prayer to receive Christ as his Savior. We all cried.

Honestly, it wasn't the words of the prayer said out loud that saved my dad; it was his realization that his sin was cause for banishment from God's presence. Dad was without hope until he surrendered to the God who loved him and who sacrificed His Son in atonement for sin. Dad's faith in Jesus saved him.

I believe that my father's outward confession of his faith that day was for my benefit, a gift from God to me. Now, no matter what the future holds, I know for sure that I will see my father in heaven, and we will spend eternity together with the One who loves us most.

Thank you, Lord, for second chances.

# Part 3

# Your Story

## Chapter Fourteen

# Have You Given Him Your Heart?

*"I have swept away your offenses like a cloud, your sins like the morning mist. Return to me, for I have redeemed you."*
Isaiah 44:22

Now that you have read Gomer's story, hopefully you were moved by the power of the final chapter in which Hosea comes for Gomer with all the splendor of a joyous wedding procession. The hope of ever experiencing such beauty and love was almost too much for Gomer to even dream of. Maybe you find yourself in the same place, laying down any hope of ever knowing the newness and joy of a pure and Godly love. Perhaps you think no one will ever come for you.

The truth is that what Hosea did for Gomer is what Christ has done for you. If you have accepted Christ as your Savior, you have a heavenly bridegroom who is coming for you. Throughout Scripture, the image of marriage is used many times, and in chapter two of the book of Mark in the Bible, Jesus even calls himself the bridegroom.

If you cannot have a do-over in this lifetime, you have a heavenly bridegroom offering you a spiritual do-over, and you can live eternally with the One who loves you most. You will be cleansed and forgiven, whole and happy, and loved for all eternity.

Let's make sure you're ready.

**Am I a sinner like Gomer?**
*"For all have sinned and fall short of the glory of God."*
Romans 3:23

**What did God do to help me in my sin?**
*"For God so loved the world that he gave his one and only son, that whoever believes in him shall not perish but have eternal life."* John 3:16

**How do I know what love is?**
*"This is how we know what love is: Jesus Christ laid down his life for us."* 1 John 3:16

**So, that makes Jesus my Redeemer, just as Hosea redeemed Gomer?**
Yes! *"For even the Son of Man did not come to be served, but to serve, and to give his life as a ransom for many."* Mark 10:45

**What must I do to be saved?**
*"If you confess with your mouth the Lord Jesus and believe in your heart that God has raised Him from the dead, you will be saved."*
Romans 10:9

**I'm not sure what to say. How do I pray?**
If you have yet to know Christ's love on a personal level, and would like to, please pray this prayer:

*Lord Jesus, I believe you are the Son of God, and that You died on the cross for my sins, rising on the third day, and redeeming my life from "the auction block." Your sacrifice has saved me from eternal torment in the fires of hell, just as Hosea paid the price to redeem Gomer from the auction block. Please forgive me, and come into my heart so that I can have new life in You. Amen.*

(If you have prayed this prayer for the first time, please seek out a local Christian Bible-based church, or a Bible-believing Christian who can continue to guide you in your new life with Christ.)

**If you are a committed Christian who has repented but is still struggling with your past, please pray this prayer:**

*Lord, you know that I am repentant of my sins against you, and I understand that you love me and have forgiven me. I am ready to let go of my past, release the guilt, and receive the healing you promised me in Your Word. Thank You for making me whole and new again. I am pure and spotless because of your redeeming love. May my actions and choices from this day forward reflect this truth! In Jesus' name, Amen.*

And so begins

# YOUR STORY.

It's time for you to start your own journey, and may you feel loved every step of the way.

# Part 4

# The End of the Story

~

Then I heard what sounded like a great multitude, like the roar of rushing waters and like loud peals of thunder, shouting:
"Hallelujah!
For our Lord God Almighty reigns.
Let us rejoice and be glad
and give him glory!
For the wedding of the Lamb has come,
and his bride has made herself ready.
Fine linen, bright and clean,
was given her to wear."
(Fine linen stands for the righteous acts of God's holy people.)

Then the angel said to me, "Write this: Blessed are those who are invited to the wedding supper of the Lamb!" And he added, "These are the true words of God."

The last book of the Bible
Revelation 19:6-9 (NIV)

# Scripture Reference

## Hosea 1-3:4

New International Version (NIV)

[1] The word of the LORD that came to Hosea son of Beeri during the reigns of Uzziah, Jotham, Ahaz and Hezekiah, kings of Judah, and during the reign of Jeroboam son of Jehoash king of Israel:

## Hosea's Wife and Children

[2] When the LORD began to speak through Hosea, the LORD said to him, "Go, marry a promiscuous woman and have children with her, for like an adulterous wife this land is guilty of unfaithfulness to the LORD." [3] So he married Gomer daughter of Diblaim, and she conceived and bore him a son.

[4] Then the LORD said to Hosea, "Call him Jezreel, because I will soon punish the house of Jehu for the massacre at Jezreel, and I will put an end to the kingdom of Israel. [5] In that day I will break Israel's bow in the Valley of Jezreel."

[6] Gomer conceived again and gave birth to a daughter. Then the LORD said to Hosea, "Call her Lo-Ruhamah (which means "not loved"), for I will no longer show love to Israel, that I should at all forgive them. [7] Yet I will show love to Judah; and I will save them —not by bow, sword or battle, or by horses and horsemen, but I, the LORD their God, will save them."

[8] After she had weaned Lo-Ruhamah, Gomer had another son. [9] Then the LORD said, "Call him Lo-Ammi (which means "not my people"), for you are not my people, and I am not your God.

[10] "Yet the Israelites will be like the sand on the seashore, which cannot be measured or counted. In the place where it was said to

them, 'You are not my people,' they will be called 'children of the living God.' [11] he people of Judah and the people of Israel will come together; they will appoint one leader and will come up out of the land, for great will be the day of Jezreel.

[2]"Say of your brothers, 'My people,' and of your sisters, 'My loved one.'

## Israel Punished and Restored

[2]"Rebuke your mother, rebuke her,
for she is not my wife,
and I am not her husband.
Let her remove the adulterous look from her face
and the unfaithfulness from between her breasts.
[3]Otherwise I will strip her naked
and make her as bare as on the day she was born;
I will make her like a desert,
turn her into a parched land,
and slay her with thirst.
[4]I will not show my love to her children,
because they are the children of adultery.
[5]Their mother has been unfaithful
and has conceived them in disgrace.
She said, 'I will go after my lovers,
who give me my food and my water,
my wool and my linen, my olive oil and my drink.'
[6]Therefore I will block her path with thornbushes;
I will wall her in so that she cannot find her way.
[7]She will chase after her lovers but not catch them;
she will look for them but not find them.
Then she will say,
'I will go back to my husband as at first,
for then I was better off than now.'
[8]She has not acknowledged that I was the one
who gave her the grain, the new wine and oil,
who lavished on her the silver and gold—
which they used for Baal.
[9]"Therefore I will take away my grain when it ripens,

and my new wine when it is ready.
I will take back my wool and my linen,
intended to cover her naked body.
¹⁰So now I will expose her lewdness
before the eyes of her lovers;
no one will take her out of my hands.
¹¹I will stop all her celebrations:
her yearly festivals, her New Moons,
her Sabbath days—all her appointed festivals.
¹²I will ruin her vines and her fig trees,
which she said were her pay from her lovers;
I will make them a thicket,
and wild animals will devour them.
¹³I will punish her for the days
she burned incense to the Baals;
she decked herself with rings and jewelry,
and went after her lovers,
but me she forgot,"
declares the LORD.

¹⁴"Therefore I am now going to allure her;
I will lead her into the wilderness
and speak tenderly to her.
¹⁵There I will give her back her vineyards,
and will make the Valley of Achor a door of hope.
There she will respond as in the days of her youth,
as in the day she came up out of Egypt.
¹⁶"In that day," declares the LORD,
"you will call me 'my husband';
you will no longer call me 'my master.'
¹⁷I will remove the names of the Baals from her lips;
no longer will their names be invoked.
¹⁸In that day I will make a covenant for them
with the beasts of the field, the birds in the sky
and the creatures that move along the ground.
Bow and sword and battle
I will abolish from the land,

so that all may lie down in safety.
¹⁹I will betroth you to me forever;
I will betroth you in righteousness and justice,
in love and compassion.
²⁰I will betroth you in faithfulness,
and you will acknowledge the LORD.

²¹"In that day I will respond,"
declares the LORD—
"I will respond to the skies,
and they will respond to the earth;
²²and the earth will respond to the grain,
the new wine and the olive oil,
and they will respond to Jezreel.
²³I will plant her for myself in the land;
I will show my love to the one I called 'Not my loved one.'
I will say to those called 'Not my people,' 'You are my people';
and they will say, 'You are my God.'"

## Hosea's Reconciliation With His Wife

¹The LORD said to me, "Go, show your love to your wife again,
though she is loved by another man and is an adulteress. Love her
as the LORD loves the Israelites, though they turn to other gods and
love the sacred raisin cakes."

²So I bought her for fifteen shekels of silver and about a homer and
a lethek of barley. ³Then I told her, "You are to live with me many
days; you must not be a prostitute or be intimate with any man, and
I will behave the same way toward you."

⁴For the Israelites will live many days without king or prince,
without sacrifice or sacred stones, without ephod or household
gods.

CPSIA information can be obtained at www.ICGtesting.com
Printed in the USA
LVOW10s0547160714

394587LV00003B/6/P